MW00933463

This Book Belongs To:

_____

Most everyone has heard of Santa Claus, but have you heard of La Befana, the Italian Christmas Witch?

In a small village in Italy, children excitedly whispered about a magical visitor.

It is January 5th, the night La Befana,
the kind old witch, swoops down
on her broomstick to visit every child's home.

Legend has it....

Long ago, La Befana lived in a tiny house in the hills of Italy.

She was known for keeping her home tidy,
sweeping her floors day after day.

One evening, three wise men, known as the Magi, came to her door to ask for directions to Bethlehem and for food and shelter.

They were following a bright star in the sky, on their way to see a special baby, the baby Jesus.

"No, I have too much work to do."
so, the wise men continued on their journey
following the star without her.

Later that night, La Befana was woken up by an unusually bright light. Startled and afraid,
she knew it was a sign to follow the Magi in search of the Baby Jesus.

She quickly packed some gifts, homemade sweets and toys, and hurried to catch up to them, but the 3 wise men were too far ahead.

From that day on, La Befana decided to search for the baby on her own, flying on her broom from house to house, leaving gifts for children in case one of them might be the baby Jesus.

Every year on the night of January 5th, La Befana continues her journey, leaving treats for good children and a small piece of coal for the naughty ones.

As the stars twinkled above, a little boy named Luca and his sister were waiting for her visit.

They left out a plate of biscotti and a glass of milk for her.

They wondered if they had been good enough all year
to receive her sweet treats.

That night, while they were asleep...

La Befana arrived on her broom, smiling at the plate of biscotti.

She munched on one before leaving a handful of treats for Luca and his sister.

With a gentle laugh, she whispered,
"Remember, I search for the special child, the baby Jesus.
Like Jesus all children are special in their own way."

The next morning....

Luca woke up and saw that La Befana had been there and left them treats. From that day on, they promised to always be kind to others, hoping she would return next year.

We will be good La Befana!
See you next year!

Made in United States
Troutdale, OR
12/28/2024

27390555R00019